PEANUTS

Let's Fly a Kite, Charlie Brown!

Peanuts® characters created and drawn by Charles M. Schulz
Text by Harry Coe Verr
Backgrounds illustrated by Art and Kim Ellis

 A GOLDEN BOOK • NEW YORI

Published in the United States by Golden Books, an imprint of Random House Children's Books, a division of Penguin Random House LLC, 1745 Broadway, New York, NY 10019, and in Canada by Random House of Canada, a division of Penguin Random House Ltd., Toronto.
Originally published by Western Publishing Company, Inc., in 1988. Golden Books, A Golden Book, A Little Golden Book, the G colophon, and the distinctive gold spine are registered trademarks of Penguin Random House LLC.
randomhousekids.com
Educators and librarians, for a variety of teaching tools, visit us at RHTeachersLibrarians.com
ISBN 978-1-101-93519-4 (trade) — ISBN 978-1-101-93520-0 (ebook)
Printed in the United States of America
10 9 8 7 6 5 4 3 2 1
Random House Children's Books supports the First Amendment and celebrates the right to read.

Spring, summer, autumn, winter . . . Charlie Brown and his friends had fun all year long! There were special things to do in every season of the year.

In springtime they flew kites.

“Oh, no!” said Charlie Brown. “Not again! My kite is stuck in a tree.”

The grass was turning green. Pretty flowers were blooming.

"Here, Schroeder," said Lucy. "I picked them myself."

Schroeder was too busy to answer.

Snoopy enjoyed the sweet spring air.

The weather grew warmer. The baseball season started.

"Pitch it to her, Charlie Brown!" called Linus. "Maybe this time you'll strike her out."

worm

Soon it was really summer. Charlie Brown and Snoopy went fishing at the lake.

Snoopy didn't take any chances!

Woodstock cooled off under the faucet.

"There's nothing like ice cream for a cool summer treat," said Linus.

"You can say that again," said Lucy.

"There's nothing like ice cream for a cool summer treat," said Linus.

Charlie Brown and Sally built a sand castle when they went to the beach.

"Finished at last!" Charlie Brown said with a sigh.

"Don't look now," said Sally, "but here comes a wave."

Summer seemed short. It wasn't long before autumn arrived. The leaves changed color and fell to the ground.

"Good grief!" said Charlie Brown. "Do we have to rake all these leaves into a pile?"

Snoopy went for a hike. Woodstock and his cousins went along.

When the air got crisp, it was time to carve scary pumpkin faces and to go trick-or-treating.

It was also time to play football.

"Please don't pull the ball away before I kick it," Charlie Brown begged Lucy.

When winter arrived, everyone played in the snow.
The pond froze. Snoopy and Charlie Brown slid without any skates.

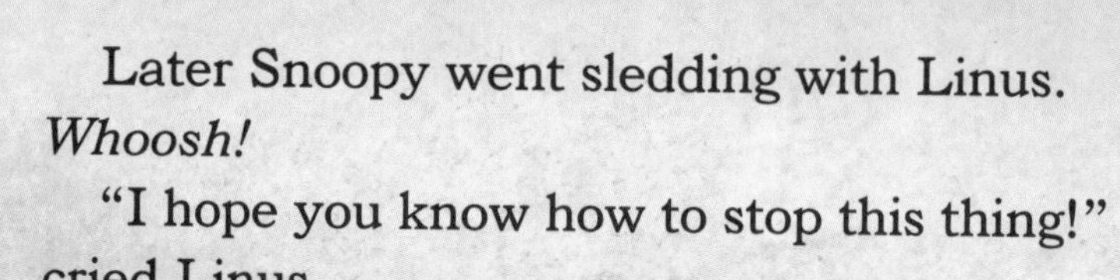

Later Snoopy went sledding with Linus. *Whoosh!*

"I hope you know how to stop this thing!" cried Linus.

Snoopy decorated his doghouse for the holidays.

And before long it was spring again.

"Let's fly a kite, Charlie Brown!" cried Charlie Brown's friends.